For Gretchen Kieling and Thomas Perkins

S.K.

One morning at school, Thomas's teacher, Mrs. Berenson, made an announcement.

"Next Monday is Valentine's Day. I want each of you to pick a name from this hat and make a valentine for the person you pick."

WILL YOU BE *Pride* MY VALENTINE?

by Steven Kroll
illustrated by Lillian Hoban

SCHOLASTIC INC.

New York   Toronto   London   Auckland   Sydney

Pride

ISBN 0-590-25609-2

Text copyright © 1993 by Steven Kroll.
Illustrations copyright © 1993 by Lillian Hoban.
All rights reserved. Published by Scholastic Inc., 555 Broadway, New York,
NY 10012, by arrangement with Holiday House, Inc.

12 11 10 9 8 7 6 5 4 3 2 1   5 6 7 8 9/9 0/0
Printed in the U.S.A.   14
First Scholastic printing, January 1995

Thomas got in line. When it was his turn, he reached down deep into the hat and smooshed the slips of paper around. Then he pulled one out.

Gretchen it said in big letters.

"Oh, wow," thought Thomas. "Oh, great!" He was so happy, he couldn't speak. Gretchen was his favorite girl in the whole class. He liked everything about her: her ponytail, her shiny neat bangs, the way she smiled.

But Gretchen didn't like Thomas. She didn't like to do any of the things he liked to do.

She didn't like building block towers because they fell down on her.

She didn't like finger painting because it was messy.

She didn't like playing in the sandbox because her dresses got dirty.

"Maybe," thought Thomas, "maybe if I make Gretchen the most beautiful valentine in the whole world, she will like me."

The moment Thomas got home from school, he began working on the valentine. He cut a big heart out of a piece of red paper. He pasted little white hearts around the edge. Carefully, he drew a picture of a boy and a girl in the middle. The boy and girl looked just like Thomas and Gretchen.

The next morning after breakfast, Thomas stuck stars all over his valentine. When his mother came in, ready to drive him to school,
she couldn't help but notice.
"Thomas," she asked,
"who are you making that beautiful valentine for?"

"Gretchen," said Thomas.
"Lucky girl," said Mom.
"I hope she'll think so," said Thomas.

He left the valentine on his desk. All the way to school, he wondered if Gretchen would be nice to him today. When he had taken off his jacket, he asked her, "Would you like to play with the trucks?"

"No, thank you," said Gretchen, "I'm making a macaroni necklace with Lisa."

A little later, Thomas asked, "Would you like to play on the jungle gym?"

"No, thank you," said Gretchen, "I'm playing on the slide with Ellie."

Later still, Thomas saw Gretchen
in the doll corner with Nancy.
He walked over and smiled.
"Hi," he said. "May I
play dolls with you?"

Gretchen put her hands
on her hips and frowned.
"Can't you see I don't like
to play with boys?"

Thomas was so upset,
he kicked over
a pile of blocks.

Then he went off in a corner
and worked on a puzzle
by himself.

When his mom came
to pick him up,
he didn't say a word.

As soon as Thomas got home, he went to his room. He took the valentine he'd almost finished for Gretchen and threw it in the wastebasket. Then he sat at his desk, folded his arms, and looked at the wall.

The next morning, Thomas's mom asked why he wasn't working on the valentine.

"Gretchen doesn't like me," said Thomas. "She's always mean to me. Could you please get her a stupid, boring old store-bought valentine?"

"I think we should invite her over," said Mom.

"She won't come."

"Let me see what I can do."

That day at school, Thomas paid no attention to Gretch-
en. He played with Bobby and Maria instead. When his
mom came to pick him up, she said, "Guess what? I've

spoken to Gretchen's mother. Gretchen is coming to play on Saturday afternoon."

"That's tomorrow," said Thomas. "I hope she won't be mean to me."

When Gretchen arrived with her mom, Thomas said, "Want to make a block castle?"

Gretchen scrunched up her nose. "Only if it's small."

"O.K.," said Thomas. "We'll build a *small* castle."

They used red blocks. And green blocks. And blue blocks. And yellow blocks. They made a little castle with towers and walls and a drawbridge.

"Now let's make a maca-
roni bracelet," said Gretchen.
"Only if I can color mine
brown," said Thomas.
"O.K.," said Gretchen.

Thomas's mom gave them
a bowl of macaroni, a box
of coloring pens, and some
pieces of yarn. Thomas col-
ored the macaroni brown.
Then he strung it on a piece
of yarn and tied the two
ends in a knot.

"Nice bracelet!" Gretchen said.

"Now it's time to make cookies," said Thomas's mom.
"Yay!" said Thomas.
"Yay!" said Gretchen.
Together they mixed the batter
and plopped the little blobs
of cookie dough on the
cookie sheets.

Then they licked
the mixing bowl.

When the cookies were ready,
Thomas's mom let each of them
have one with a glass of milk.

Finally, it was time for Gretchen to go home. Her mother came to pick her up.

"Bye," Gretchen said, "I had fun. See you Monday in school."

When she had gone, Thomas raced to his room and pulled Gretchen's valentine out of the wastebasket. He added more white hearts around the edge. He drew a bunch of flowers at the bottom.

Then he asked his mom to write *Will you be my valentine?* across the top.

"I guess you and Gretchen had a good time," said Mom.

"I think she likes me now," said Thomas.

Monday was Valentine's Day. As soon as all the children had arrived at school, Mrs. Berenson said, "First we're going to exchange valentines. Then we'll have our party."

Everyone seemed to be moving at once. A little girl called Holly rushed up and gave Thomas a valentine. Before Thomas could reach Gretchen, Gretchen gave one to Harrison. Then Harrison gave Gretchen a valentine!

Gretchen smiled and took it. She and Harrison sat down next to Ellie.

Thomas couldn't believe what he'd seen. *He* had chosen Gretchen's name. *He* was supposed to give her a valentine! Why had Harrison given her one? Did he like Gretchen, too?

Maybe Thomas was wrong about Saturday. Maybe nothing had changed after all. Maybe Gretchen still didn't like him. Maybe she liked Harrison instead.

Thomas stalked over to Gretchen and handed her his Valentine.

"Thank you, Thomas," she said. Then she giggled and looked at Harrison.

That did it! Thomas stormed across the room and sat down next to Bobby. He was so upset, he didn't even want any valentine cookies and punch.

When it was almost time to go home, Gretchen came
running up to him.

"There you are!" she said.
"I've been waiting to give
you this *secret* valentine."

Thomas shrugged. "I thought Harrison was your valentine."

"That was a mistake. He got mixed up. His card was supposed to be for Ellie."

"Oh," said Thomas. He opened the envelope. Inside was a piece of folded cardboard with a heart on each side. Under one heart it said *Gretchen*. Under the other it said *Thomas*.

"You're my valentine," said Gretchen.
"You're mine, too," said Thomas.
"Happy Valentine's Day!" said Gretchen.
"Happy Valentine's Day!" said Thomas.